Specs for Rex

Yasmeen Ismail

BLOOMSBURY
LONDON NEW DELHI NEW YORK SYDNEY

Rex had new specs.

Rex's specs were BIG
and ROUND and RED.

Rex did NOT like his
specs . . . AT ALL!

At breakfast time, Rex tried to hide his glasses, but Daddy heard all the crinkling and crunching.

"Put those glasses
back on, Rex,"
he said.

Mummy and Rex walked together to school.
"Have a fun day, Rexy," said Mummy.
"I'll see you soon."
And she kissed him bye-bye.

As soon as Mummy had gone, Rex brushed his hair over his face.
At least no one would be able to see his glasses now.

But it was Rex who couldn't see anything!
He stumbled into the classroom.

"Rex!" cried Miss Spots. "What a racket!
Take your hair out of your face
and come and sit down."

"Play nicely, children," said Miss Spots.
"Now, where HAS my whistle gone?"

While all the other children played, Rex hid.
He didn't want anyone to see his stupid specs.

At snack-time, Rex found the perfect hiding place for his glasses.

But he was too hungry. Soon his hiding place had been gobbled up.

In Art, Miss Spots asked them to paint a picture.

Rex painted his specs.

"Now they're sunglasses!"
Rex mumbled to himself.

He's funny!
thought Zoe.

"Oh Rex," Miss Spots groaned.

She sent Rex to the bathroom to wash his face.

Rex had an idea.

They all ran into the playground.
It was pretty windy outside!

Everyone had fun playing
chase with Rex.

After break, they all pretended to be jumping beans.
Except for Rex. He found another way of hiding his specs –
and he found something else, too!

"Here's your whistle, Miss!" said Rex.

"Oh, well spotted, Rex!" said Miss Spots.
"I think that earns you a gold star.
Those new glasses of yours must be working!"

When it was home time, they went to the cloakroom to get their coats.

"I like your specs, Rex!" chirped Zoe.
"I'm going to ask my mummy if I can have glasses too!
Can you come and play at my house tomorrow?"

Rex's mummy was waiting for him.
"So, how were your new specs?"
she asked, giving him a big hug.

"They were great!" beamed Rex.
"They helped me find Miss Spots'
whistle and I got a gold star!"

"Oh, that's wonderful!" said Mummy.
"That deserves the biggest hug EVER!"

For three silly monkeys, Kai, Ayeishah and Lila.

A big thank you to Zoe W. and Alison R. for their unwavering support, hard work, splendid ideas and encouragement! It's been wonderful working with you both on this book.
Congratulations to Emma B. on her new baby,
and thanks to Vicki W.L. and Bloomsbury for their continued advocacy,
and to Alasdair, for always cooking delicious things and being so terrifically supportive.

~YI

Bloomsbury Publishing, London, New Delhi, New York and Sydney

First published in Great Britain in 2014 by Bloomsbury Publishing Plc
50 Bedford Square, London, WC1B 3DP

A CIP catalogue record for this book is available from the British Library

ISBN 978 1 4088 3696 5 (HB)
ISBN 978 1 4088 3697 2 (PB)
ISBN 978 1 4088 3957 7 (eBook)

Printed in China by Leo Paper Products, Heshan, Guangdong

1 3 5 7 9 10 8 6 4 2

www.bloomsbury.com